Come Play with Me

by Nell Wynn-Thomas

Illustrated by Normand L. Chartier

 HOUGHTON MIFFLIN   BOSTON • MORRIS PLAINS, NJ

California   •   Colorado   •   Georgia   •   Illinois   •   New Jersey   •   Texas

"Come play with me,"
said Pig.

"Not I," said Hen.

"Come play with me,"
said Pig.

4

"Not I," said Cat.

5

"Come play with me,"
said Pig.

6

"Not I," said Dog.

"Then I will play," said Pig.